Dr Clement C. Moore was born in New York in 1779. He was a Professor of Hebrew and Greek, but today his name is best remembered as the writer of this poem. Composed in 1822 for his six children, it was first published as **A Visit from St Nicholas** in 1823 and has since been published in many languages and versions.

ISBN 978-1-84135-796-6

Illustrations copyright © Award Publications Limited

All rights reserved

This edition first published 2010

Published by Award Publications Limited,
The Old Riding School, The Welbeck Estate,
Worksop, Nottinghamshire, S80 3LR

10 1

Printed in China

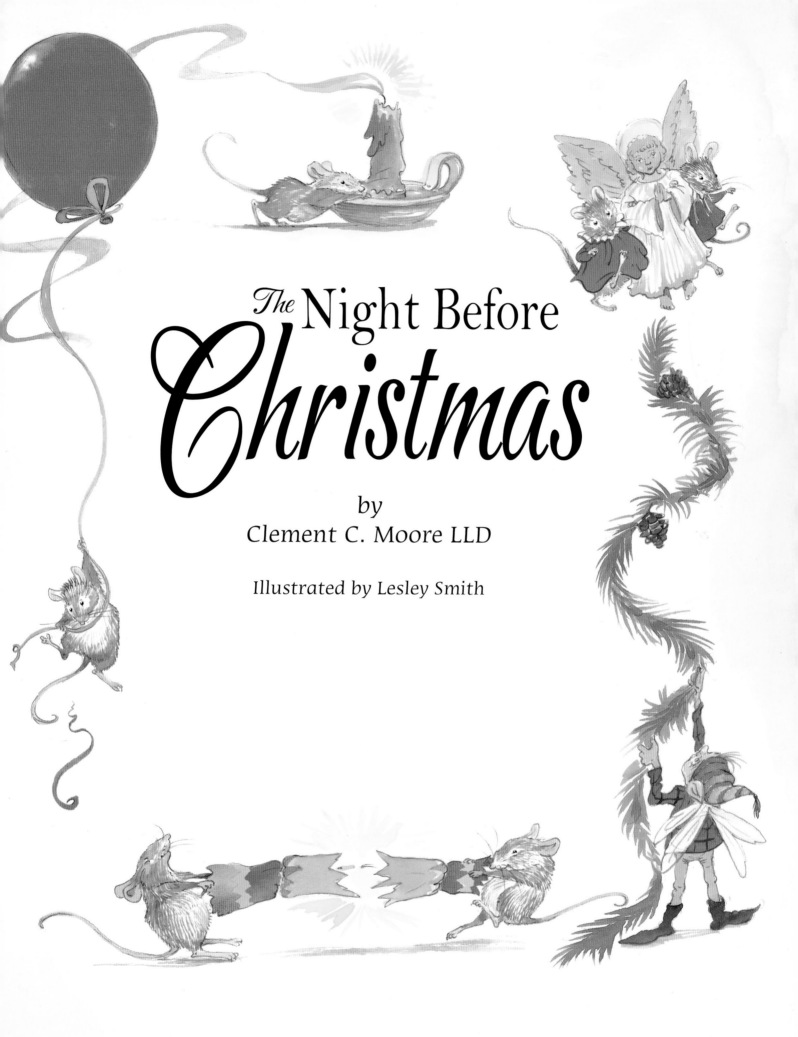

The Night Before Christmas

by
Clement C. Moore LLD

Illustrated by Lesley Smith

AWARD PUBLICATIONS LIMITED

'Twas the night before Christmas,
  when all through the house
Not a creature was stirring,
  not even a mouse;
The stockings were hung by
  the chimney with care,
In hopes that St Nicholas
  soon would be there;

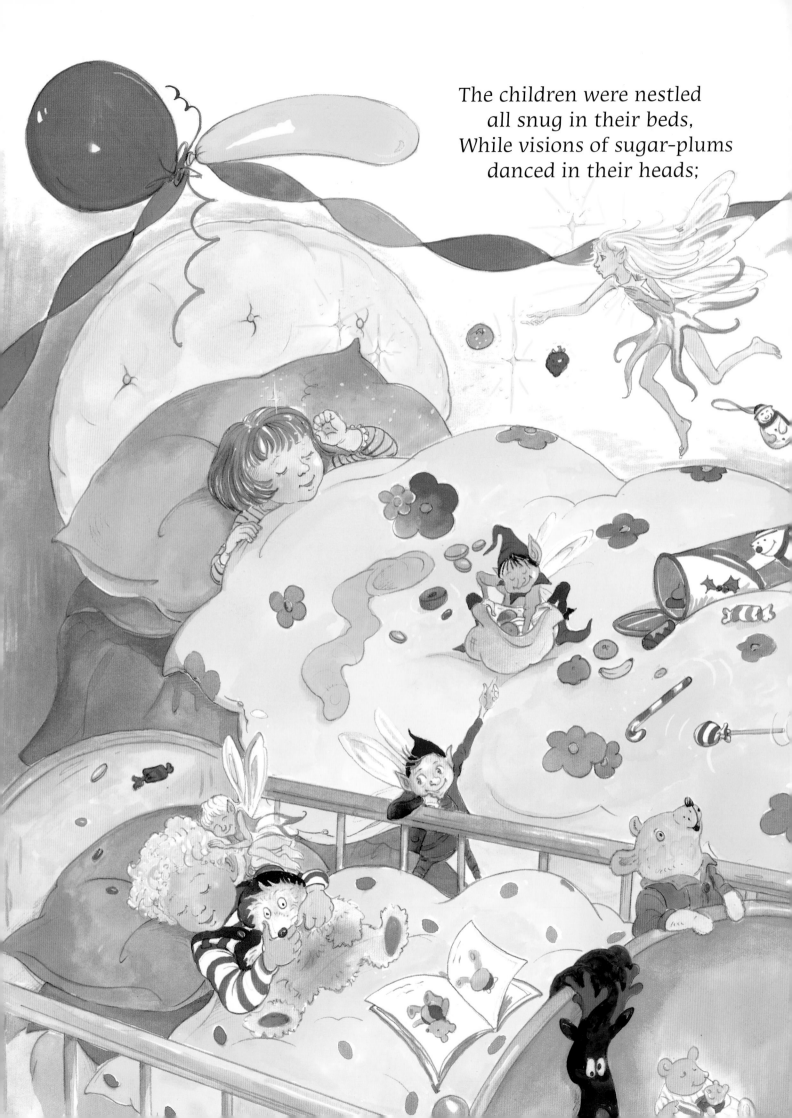

The children were nestled
all snug in their beds,
While visions of sugar-plums
danced in their heads;

And Mamma in her kerchief,
and I in my cap,
Had just settled our brains
for a long winter's nap;

When out on the lawn
there arose such a clatter,
I sprang from the bed
to see what was the matter.

Away to the window
I flew like a flash,
Tore open the shutters
and threw up the sash.

The moon on the breast
of the new-fallen snow,
Gave lustre of midday
to objects below.

When what to my wondering
eyes should appear,
But a miniature sleigh and
eight tiny reindeer,
With a little old driver,
so lively and quick,
I knew in a moment
it must be St Nick.

More rapid than eagles
his coursers they came,
And he whistled and shouted,
and called them by name:
"Now, Dasher! now, Dancer!
now, Prancer and Vixen!
On, Comet! on, Cupid!
on, Donner and Blitzen!

"To the top of the porch,
    to the top of the wall!
Now dash away! dash away!
    dash away all!"
As dry leaves that before
    the wild hurricane fly,
When they meet with an obstacle,
    mount to the sky,
So up to the housetop
    the coursers they flew,
With the sleigh full of toys,
    and St Nicholas too.

And then in a twinkling
    I heard on the roof
The prancing and pawing
    of each little hoof.
As I drew in my head,
    and was turning around,
Down the chimney St Nicholas
    came with a bound.

He was dressed all in fur
from his head to his foot,
And his clothes were all tarnished
with ashes and soot;

A bundle of toys he had
flung on his back,
And he looked like a pedlar
just opening his pack.

His eyes – how they twinkled!
　　his dimples, how merry!
His cheeks were like roses,
　　his nose like a cherry!
His droll little mouth
　　was drawn up like a bow,
And his beard on his chin
　　was as white as the snow.
The stump of a pipe
　　he held tight in his teeth,
And the smoke it encircled
　　his head like a wreath.

He had a broad face
    and a little round belly,
That shook, when he laughed,
    like a bowl full of jelly.
He was chubby and plump,
    a right jolly old elf;
And I laughed when I saw him,
    in spite of myself.

A wink of his eye and a
twist of his head
Soon gave me to know
I had nothing to dread.

He spoke not a word,
but went straight to his work,
And filled all the stockings;
then turned with a jerk.

And laying his finger aside
    of his nose,
And giving a nod, up the
    chimney he rose.

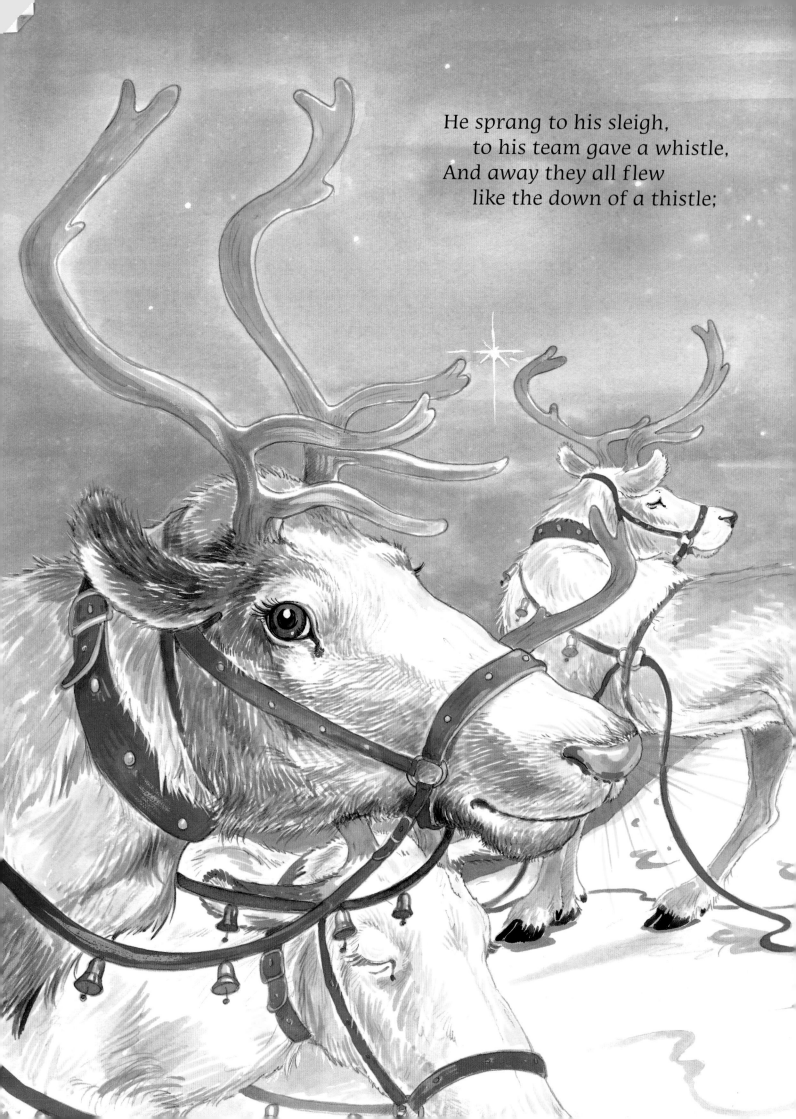

He sprang to his sleigh,
   to his team gave a whistle,
And away they all flew
   like the down of a thistle;

But I heard him exclaim,
    ere he drove out of sight,
"Happy Christmas to all,
    and to all a good night!"